Our Super Solar System

Linda Jacobson

INFOMAX
COMMON CORE
READERS

Rosen Classroom™

New York

Published in 2013 by The Rosen Publishing Group, Inc.
29 East 21st Street, New York, NY 10010

Book Design: Michael Harmon

Photo Credits: Cover © iStockphoto.com/adventtr; p. 4 Hemera/Thinkstock.com; p. 5 Thinkstock Images/Thinkstock.com; p. 6 vectomart/Shutterstock.com; p. 7 Gregor Kervina/Shutterstock.com; p. 8 Triff/Shutterstock.com; p. 9 biletskiy/Shutterstock.com; p. 10 Photodisc/Photodisc/Getty Images; p. 11 World Perspectives/Stone/Getty Images; p. 12 rangizz/Shutterstock.com; p. 13 Adastra/Taxi/Getty Images; p. 14 (asteroid) Stocktrek/Photodisc/Getty Images; p. 14 (asteroid belt) iStockphoto/Thinkstock.com; pp. 15, 21 Byron W.Moore/Shutterstock.com; p. 16 Jason Reed/Photodisc/Getty Images; p. 17 Luis Stortini aka CVADRAT/Shutterstock.com; p. 18 © iStockphoto.com/larslentz; p. 19 Diego Barucco/Shutterstock.com; p. 20 a. v. ley/Shutterstock.com.

ISBN: 978-1-4488-9070-5
6-pack ISBN: 978-1-4488-9071-2

Manufactured in the United States of America

CPSIA Compliance Information: Batch #WS12RC: For further information contact Rosen Publishing, New York, New York at 1-800-237-9932.

Word Count: 500

Contents

What's a Solar System?

Earth seems very big to us. However, it's only one small part of a huge solar system. Our solar system is made up of the sun and the things that move around it.

There are eight planets in our solar system. Planets are large bodies in space that move around the sun. Earth is one of these planets.

Everything in the solar system moves in a path around the sun. These paths are called orbits. Earth takes one year to make one orbit around the sun.

Many planets have smaller bodies that move around them. These are called moons. Earth has one moon. You can see it in the sky.

The Sun

The sun is the **center** of our solar system. It's a huge star. The sun is made of gases that are very hot. The sun's hottest part is its **core**.

The sun sends **energy** to the planets in the solar system. It gives us light and heat on Earth. Plants use sunlight to make food. They take in sunlight through their leaves.

Mercury and Venus

The closest planet to the sun is Mercury. It has the shortest orbit of all the planets. It takes Mercury only 88 days to travel once around the sun.

Venus is the second planet from the sun. It's a very hot planet. There are more than a thousand **volcanoes** on Venus!

Our Planet

Earth is the third planet from the sun. The water on Earth helps things live and grow. Earth is the only planet known to have plants, animals, and people.

The Red Planet

Mars is the fourth planet from the sun. It's called the Red Planet because it has red **soil**. There are storms on Mars that blow the planet's soil around!

The Asteroid Belt and Beyond

Asteroids (AS-tuh-royds) are large pieces of rock that orbit the sun. Many asteroids share an orbit in a part of the solar system called the asteroid belt.

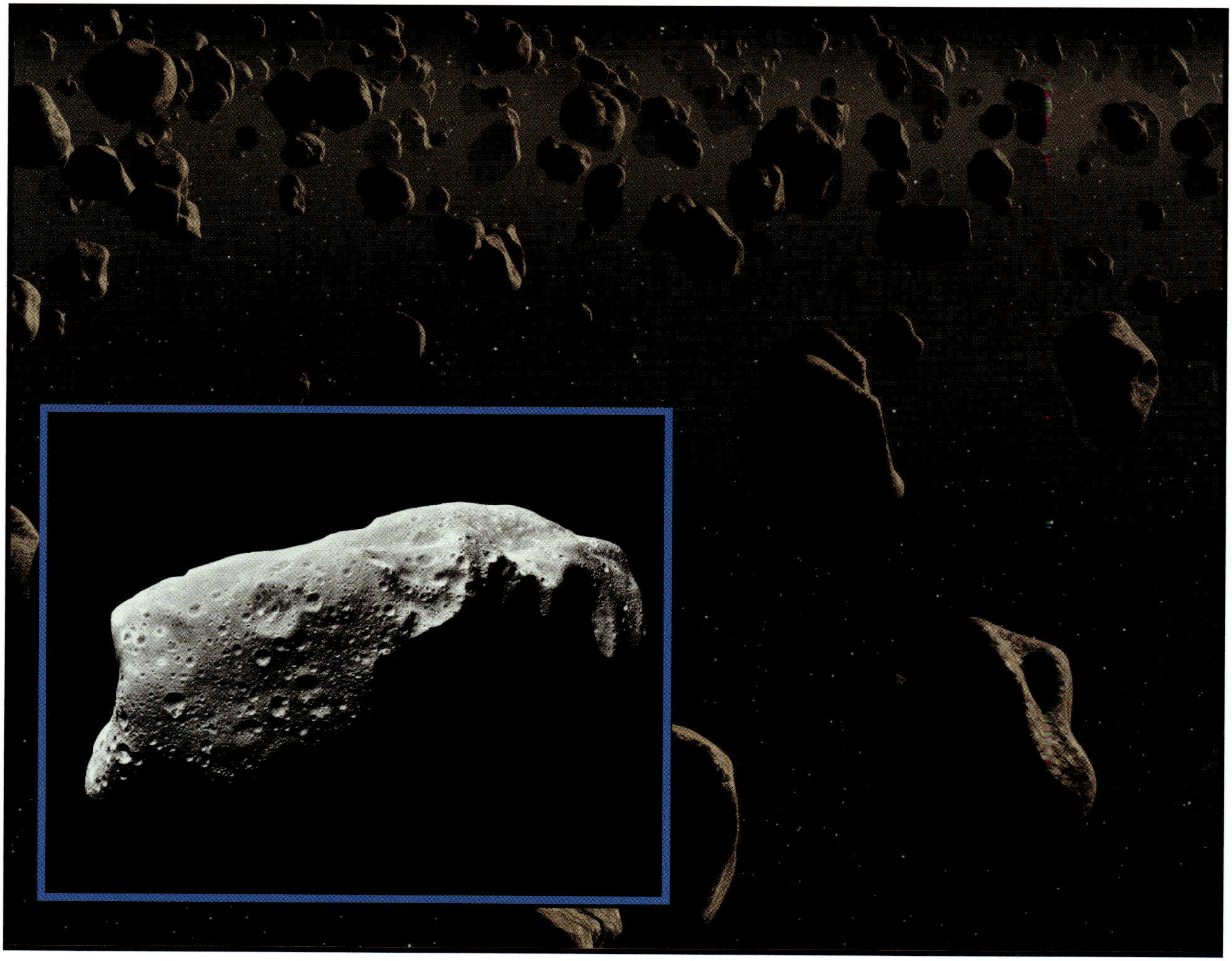

Jupiter is the first planet beyond the asteroid belt. It's the largest planet in our solar system. It's made of different gases. There's a huge storm on Jupiter. It's called the Great Red Spot.

Saturn is the sixth planet in our solar system. It's made of gases, too. Jupiter and Saturn both have many moons.

Saturn is known for its rings. They're mostly made of big and small pieces of ice. The ice has its own orbit around Saturn. You can see these rings from space!

Uranus is the seventh planet in our solar system. It's made of gases that give it a blue-green color. It has rings, too. People have discovered 11 rings around Uranus.

Neptune is the farthest planet from the sun. It has the longest orbit. Neptune is made of gases, too. The gases give it a bright blue color.

Cool Comets

Comets are balls of rock and ice. They form beyond Neptune. Comets get tails that glow as they move around the sun.

Dwarf Planets

Some bodies that orbit the sun are too small to be called planets but too big to be asteroids. They're **dwarf** planets. Pluto is a dwarf planet.

A Map of Our Solar System

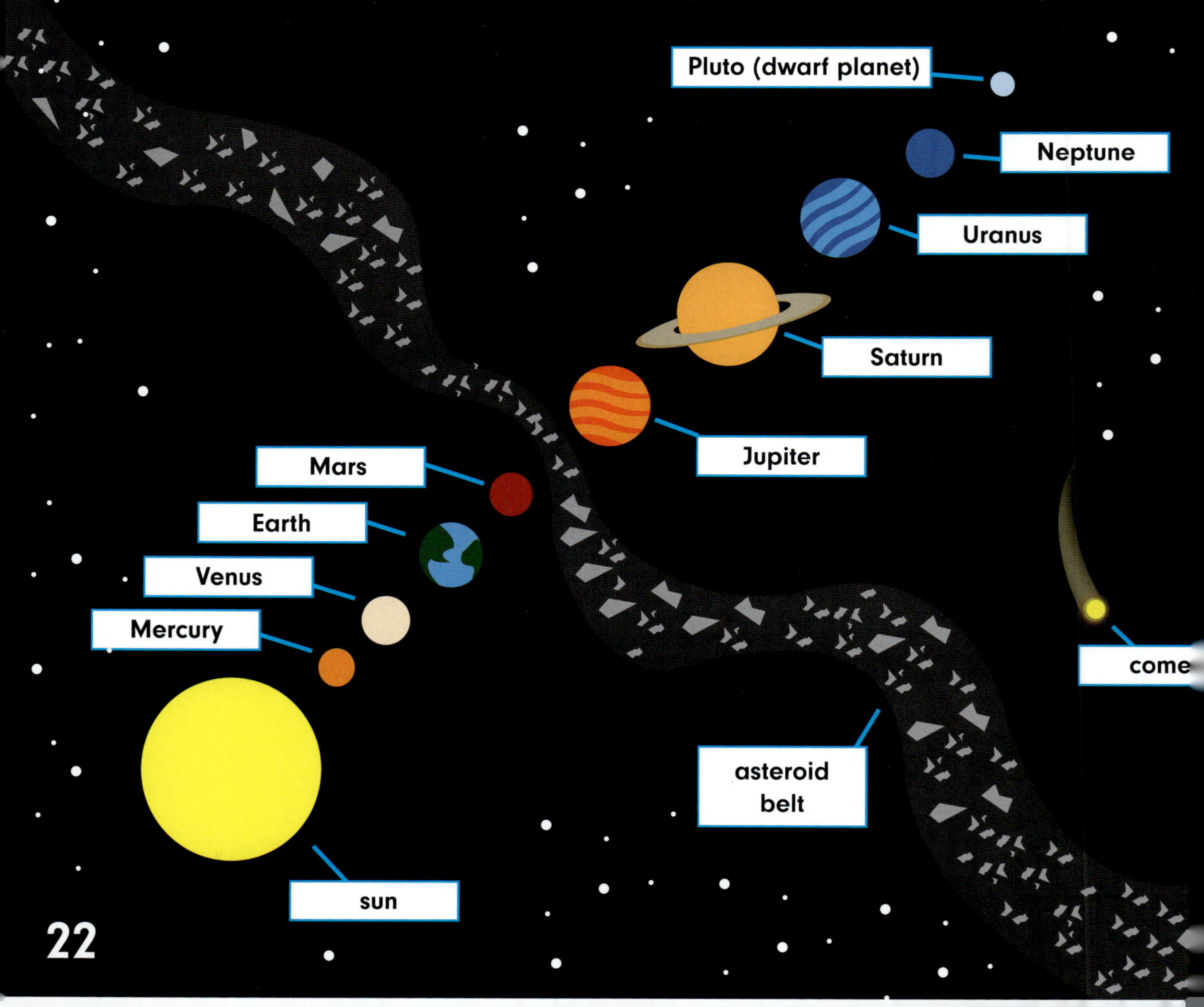

Glossary

center (SEHN-tuhr) Middle.

core (KOHR) The center part inside something.

dwarf (DWORF) Something that is much smaller than others of its kind.

energy (EH-nuhr-jee) Power.

soil (SOYL) Dirt.

volcano (vohl-KAY-noh) An opening in the ground where hot gases and flowing rock come out.

Index